The Killing of Perry Santos and Other Stories

Scott Durham

ISBN-13:
978-0615870427 (Padova Publishing)

ISBN-10:
0615870422

DEDICATED TO

M'Liss Inman

CONTENTS

Special thank you to Zach Scardino, and to
Christohper A. Gross, without whom this book
could not have been written.

THE MIRACLE OF SAINT BRICE

My luck has always turned grey in October. I get very sleepy and the time drags by like a plow in the sand. I have taken to renaming the month "Noctober" since I seem to miss most of it lost in a hazy slumber.

When I get hungry during these periods I do the bare minimum for nutrition, anything more than microwaving a hot dog would tire me out. It can be exhausting work maintaining my expertise at being a lummox, but I give every effort possible. The couch and has no chance of flying away, my supine protection guarantees that. The television becomes incapable of surprises as I scan its contents top to bottom. Not helping matters at all, baseball winds down to an end and I just can't help the deflation that overcomes me. This year, the lethargy continued through the first two weeks of November.

I couldn't even drag myself to the Horse Races. The empty cold devoured all my inspiration.

I heard the brass louver clink open and the sound of at least two crisply edged envelopes clacking the wood floor. The Saturday mail included a ticket to St. Catherine's Church for a neighborhood supper. This news elicited the first smile of the Noctober season. It was looking like my sacred hibernation would come to an end with the Feast of Saint Brice.

There was a certainty of going as long as it didn't interfere with my proper schedule of napping. Joy of double joys when I saw that I would be able to attend. I cleaned and pressed my suit to at least pay reverence to a free meal. Being a pauper as well as a lummox, I could not contribute more than a few cents to the prayer fund. Being a world-class professional lummox drains all of my capital. I suppose I will drop some of my smallest change in to the prayer box, along with a heavy 2 inch washer to make a big splash in the pile of darkened coinage. If it becomes necessary, I guess I'll spend a minute talking with Rose Hagerman in order to seem social without answering an interrogation. Mrs. Hagerman doesn't speak very much because she is old and always really tired and it doesn't matter what I say, she always smiles back at me.

I wish a lot more people could behave like Rose. If I said I was going for any other reason than the free food, I'd be lying. The truth is I wouldn't be caught dead inside of a church while the churching was going on.

The Feast of St. Brice is big around these parts, on account of Father Julian being a Frenchman.

That's what I always heard growing up. I can't say I know why that is the reason because I'm not much into geography or history. Our neighbor Mr. Jorgenson was a custodian at the diocese and when he would visit my father he would tell a lot of stories about Catholic stuff. I guess you could say I'm an expert on everything that goes on there. My dad never let us go to church because he said it was corrupt, just a front for begging. A real man doesn't need a hand out, he'd say. He liked Fred Jorgenson though, and I was allowed to play with all the Jorgy kids growing up so I learned Catholic stuff from them too.

Another thing I can't say is that I know why people go to church when there's better things to do. There hasn't been a miracle in 2,000 years or something like that. So many other good things can be done instead of going to church. On second thought I guess it is a nice clean place for strangers to meet and become friends and such. There's nothing wrong with having a place to meet like-minded people who could wind up being friends, if you're into that kind of thing.

Mrs. Hagerman doesn't attend the church either; she used to go to a Jewish church in the neighborhood. She can't go anymore because they relocated a while back and it is too far away from her retirement home. She is kind of in the same boat as me, a stranger to the cause. As the dinner hour approached, I heard a gurgle from my abdomen; no food was in there at all. St. Brice would be filling me up all by himself.

If I were going to join a church, it would

probably be St. Catherine's but my father would howl. It is worth a mention that the San Gennaro weekend is very special too. We have a lot of Italians in the neighborhood so there is no way of missing out on that feast. Father Julian knows me by name and knows my father too. Dad hasn't been to San Gennaro festival for a long time though; he just can't bear all the religious company anymore.

At most of these functions, there is a spirit of recruitment. Father Julian always comes to our table and shakes our hands. I would never want to be a spectacle of rudeness so I oblige the semi-annual hand shake. I hoped to get there early enough to sit next to Mrs. Hagerman. If I happened to sit next the Garbiani family again, I might have to call the evening short. They are really nice, it's the kids that run around the tables and throw napkins and little bits of food that ruin everything for me.

I walked at a brisk pace; developing the kind of appetite where you swear you could eat a raw potato in four bites. I am talking about major hunger here.

The feast meant that I was able to put away rations for two meals previous to this and will skip two more after. The Feast of St. Brice always comes to the rescue in a timely manner.

As I stepped onto the property, the buildings were all aglow at dusk. Inside the cathedral, candles gave a cherry and amber colored hue to the windows and the frescoes. I had to pace along the red carpet between the pews and turn right in front of the altar. After turning right, it was a mere convenience that the confessionals were on the left side of the foyer as you make your way to the recreation hall where the feast was held.

I often thought of trying my hand at confession, even though I hadn't had a communion or anything. I just thought it would be cool to find out if I really was a sinner like dad said I was.

Why couldn't a normal person or an agnostic confess their sins? Every sin is a sin, being Catholic won't change that much. Guilt is universally known, there must be a non-denominational variance that I can ask for to give my confession.

The urge got the best of me and I entered a vestibule.

I sat calmly for a few minutes wondering when it would start. I thought of all the stories Lyle Jorgenson told me growing up. He said there was dusty smell to the enclosure; I thought that was a strange observation. I wanted to know if they were allowed to hit you or whip you through the window.

"Hello?" I heard nothing back. Then I heard a faint thump, a door closed somewhere and suddenly the screen slid open and I heard a bible opening through the obscured mesh in the partition. I could smell the dust of 60 years on the screen in the window between us. I could tell he was not facing the window; his voice was quiet and distant. "Hello father…" I shot out.

"How long has it been since your last confession my son?"

I wondered if he knew me by voice.

"This is my first, Father is it okay if I haven't had communion yet? I just wanted to see how bad a sinner I am, my dad says I am a bad one."

"And how do you see yourself? Do you see a sinner in the mirror my son?"

The Pastor was calm and so far, had none of the corrupt arrogance that dad had said they all possessed.

"I see a nice guy trying to do his best to not be a pest to my fellow man. I don't see a sin in any of that." I was honest when I said that.

"Are you a giving person my son? Do you ever help your fellow man even when it is of no profit for you to do so?" The Father was ringing a bell for a donation, I thought.

"I am sure that whatever good I have done on my own, I did not cost another his goods or possessions. I earn my own way."

"And are you wealthy my son?" Have you gained riches and do you sleep well knowing you've done all you can for the greater good?"

"Father, you keep asking two questions at a time, it's hard to answer…"

He sounded a bit more resolute, "I ask only what your conscience would ask."

The priest was tenacious. I offered a meek justification;

"But I am a good person even though I don't share my time with others."

"Did you have any sins you'd like to confess? I can see about putting you in a catechism education program too if that is what you would like."

"I don't know Father; I think I would like to just admit to having stolen a bag of rice when I was hungry. I went to the store and bought something small and I kept the rice under my jacket all the way out. I never went back and paid for it either."

"You cannot un-commit that sin; it is a clear violation of one of the most important of God's commandments."

"I know Father, but I was young and stupid. I was very hungry and I only took what I needed, the guilt of that sin keeps me from going there again."

"You are saying you now have control over that urge, my son?" I detected a tone of authority. "Urges are a tricky thing, when God is involved."

I was not one to start an argument, but I sure could finish one. I was rattled and confused about why I went in there to begin with. I punted, "My dad says that you Catholics spend too much money on churches and don't give enough to the poor."

"Your father is gambling cheat and an adulterous misanthrope." He asserted.

"You don't know my-"

"I know well who you are and I know even better why you are trying to talk around your sins, it is much easier to not have to repent for something if you don't really have any faith in goodness." He left me speechless.

"Hey, you can't..." I didn't even get the rest of that sentence into my mouth before it was spiked into the sand behind me.

"I would never divulge the contents of your father's confession, had he ever given one." His pauses were punctually holding my attention with magnetic power. There was no plugging up this dam, he rallied onward.

"I hate to see you hold up Frank Morgan as a standard for moral achievement. You are his son, yes, but also you are a son of God and you must relent to His will, His grace and it is His forgiveness you seek, not mine. I may be corrupt and I may be arrogant as your father would say, but I am true to my word when I say, Robert Morgan repent your sins and come out of the dark, that is a message incapable of corruption!"

I angered him something fierce, I wondered if this meant that I could not attend the dinner, it was clear that he knew me by my voice.

"I am sorry Father, I meant no disrespect-"

"That's alright, I am sure you are wondering about the dinner tonight, please attend and fill yourself with the good food and delightful conversation, try not to make any trouble Bobby"

"Thank you Father- and, I am sorry if I made you mad, Sir. Father, sorry."

He was gracious to hear my rants and still allow me admittance to the feast.

When I walked in to the buffet line, I noticed that the tables were empty.

No Mrs. Hagerman.

"Where's Mrs. H?" My query was offered as a public volley, I hoped somebody could explain her tardiness.

"Oh, Bobby…" Mr. Hinton interrupted the silence, "She is at Mid-Atlantic General."

"Yeah? What happened, is she alright?" I was shocked but soon, my logic rode up beside me. I realized that at her age, her health, and her finances, she was in more need of a great free meal than I.

"Broken hip, broken arm too." Mrs. Hinton answered.

I was suddenly very sad, like maybe it was my own mother who had stood me up.

"Where's Father Julian?" I wasn't asking, I was telling.

One of the Sisters responded that he was still praying in the residence, not to be disturbed.

I had to disturb him.

"I just talked to him a moment ago, I don't think he'd mind." I really didn't think he would mind.

I walked back out to the Cathedral and went straightway into the confessional, it took longer this time, but he did come back in and slide the screen open.

"Bobby I have to get ready for the evening's activities, I can't be in here with you all night." He sounded resolute again.

"I was noticing Mrs. Hagerman is not here and I wanted to take her a dinner." I was nervous to sound like a do-gooder.

"Bobby I think that would be just fine, I can go along after you eat, we should eat first, the two of us, and then go visit her." Suddenly the Father and I were in a conspiracy of food, the words "unholy alliance" scrolled across ticker tape of my mind.

This was a good feeling, knowing that I would save her St. Brice's Day. I knew she counted on the providence of these meals like I did.

When I got my plate finally, I noticed Father Julian coming my way. He sat across from me, next to the Hintons. I ate most of my lasagna and several buttered rolls, the only thing left was an amazing salad. The lasagna sat like a shipwreck at the bottom of a clear reef. There was a subtle tide inside my stomach rolling back and forth. Salad would be pushing my luck.

"Bobby, did you get enough?" He was sincerely seeing to my satisfaction. I was more than impressed by his authenticity as a human. I like this feeling of goodness, not nearly as bad as my dad made it out to be.

"Father, I am hitting a wall here. I thought I might make up a plate to take over." I felt so odd being charitable.

"The sisters have already prepared a parcel and a dinner plate for us to take," He turned to the Hintons, "Bobby and I are gonna visit Mrs. Hagerman over at MA General."

After we both finished up and took our plates and cups to the trash bin we made our way down to Mid-Atlantic hospital.

"Father I always wondered why Mrs. Hagerman comes to St. Catherine's when she is Jewish." I didn't even know if my question was offensive or not.

"Bobby, she is a child of God and as such, I welcome her and any other friend of goodness to our suppers."

I was genuinely confused, "When the synagogue moved away, I felt like they abandoned her."

"They did not abandon her, in a small way it is St. Catherine's responsibility to take in the spiritual orphans that are left about in such misfortunes."

"My dad always said that she was just too lazy to walk an extra five blocks."

"Bobby, I find your washers in the prayer box every six months and I still think to myself, 'at least he wants to appear to be a Christian', which is more than I can say for Frank."

I defended my dad previously, but now I was seeing a different side of charity. I was seeing a different view of my father too. Dad was the example of arrogance for sure, maybe not corrupt except for imparting corrupted information.

"Mrs. Hagerman made that choice for herself, according to her conscience and her beliefs and it isn't up to me to make the whole world into Catholics." His resolute tone reappeared, almost sermon-like.

"When Christ touches a heart, I am there to guide and instruct."

"But she doesn't have Christ in her church, so how can you relate to her?"

"Charity makes for strange bedfellows my son, strange indeed - look at us!"

We laughed and rounded the last corner and went into the lobby, the elevators were waiting for us. On the ride up, he asked me to be on my best behavior.

"Look, I know my reputation is kind of skunky. I am trying to be better Father, I think I am embarrassed now at some of my past deeds but I will do better, maybe not in church, but I will be a better man from now on."

He seemed to believe me and he patted me on the shoulder, giving it a friendly squeeze. "Bobby, some of my most faithful parishioners can't learn what you are learning right now." His hand fell away and wiped at a tear that slowly stuck beneath his eye. He was smiling like I just got a trophy.

"Mrs. Hagerman? Miss Rose?" we lightly

offered.

Her room was quiet and somewhat dim. I think she was sleeping but her voice cracked as we came around her bed and into view.

"Father…Bobby, you two remembered me on St. Brice's, how thoughtful."

Her excitement was short lived as the intern came in and took away our plate, saying that the food would hurt her more than help.

"That's alright; I never go for the food anyway Father." Rose was feeling feisty.

"Mrs. Hagerman you have not missed a St. Brice's day feast since I came to this Parish, how can you say you never liked the food?"

"It was the conversations, the relationships, I loved having company to eat with" She made me feel like I would start crying. I always patronized her and made rude insensitive comments in her presence. The fool I have been in my youth!

"I was looking forward to eating with you, I couldn't let you go without the lasagna and a few rolls" I said to her.

"I have to be on a special diet until I am in the clear again." She was weak and frail; she spoke at a firm whisper.

"Doctor says I could have another stroke so they have to monitor my food"

As I sat and listened to Father Julian and her discuss neighborhood goings on, I chuckled at this bizarre encounter with the force of goodness.

I still would never be caught dead in church, but I must say that it isn't as evil as my dad always told me it was.

I guess I should give thanks to Saint Brice, the anonymous saint who brought me to understand charity and goodness. I will have to read up on this guy, this Saint Brice. Maybe Father Julian can impart some wisdom on the subject. At least we'll have more to talk about at the San Gennaro a few months from now.

A SOUVENIR FROM BALTIMORE

A cold front arrived as a nice surprise back in September. A month later it hasn't let up. Sometime last week my days became a frosty blur, the nights left me in a siege against the brisk chill outside. When the wind turned hard as steel, it was hard to do a week on the docks. I still worked in the 'rotation' but it was only a matter of time before I got to step up and into a Union gig. My brother Mickey made his way up, he's a dock supervisor. He has an office and can basically stay in there on cold days. When it's 14 degrees outside, that can be a benefit. The rotation sucked because everyone on the docks just wanted to drive the trucks, to be on the road. Too many other guys wanted the same thing and this worked to a great advantage to the Union.

With three guys fighting for every position, they had the pick of the litter. They could pay what they wanted to, even though the pay was really good. I might seem to be complaining, but really I just wish I didn't have to alternate weeks in and out of the trucks. It's not like I don't make a good living out on Pier 15, the Union sees that we all do. Sometimes I think it would be nice to know exactly who I was working for. I guess I was lucky that I even knew about the Union.

If it wasn't for my dad and my brother Mickey, we would probably just be working at the docks. When you work for the "Union" you don't "just work on the docks". Most of the guys just thought they were working for Mr. Ryan. Old man Ryan answered to "upstairs" and those were the guys who ran the entire harbor in one way or another. Either by proxy, or by influence from banks, they guided each of the angles that the harbor's economy rested upon. Companies that did well, did so at the whims of the Union.

Cagliari Transport has been slowly dying for the last two years due to a beef with Mr. Ryan. One of their Chinese vessels took on some water and that damage spread out over ten percent of the load. Cagliari had almost no insurance for this. They now had to find a way to replace the freight to their expecting suppliers. The Union claimed a loss on the whole load, their insurance was deep. Cagliari sent a guy over to inquire and adjust the deal.

Mr. Ryan did not like this. As a result the owners of Cagliari ended up paying off claims for freight that was most likely double-sold by the Union anyway.

It's a good racket. After you are in for tenure,

they pay you for two jobs. We call this a 'Union' job and to get one, is to practically be made. This morning I was walking through icy winds trying to get to work without freezing.

Inside the office at Priority East Coast Imports, the drivers assembled for the morning dispatch. A free pot of coffee and the sound of the lifts outside gave a commotion to the proceedings.

Mr. Ryan tore a sheet of paper from his legendary notebook and pinned it up to the message board.

"Seven drivers received complaints yesterday, which means *every* driver here owes me 10 bucks, cough it up-NOW." Old man Ryan was an asthmatic, he was also a mild to moderate spitter, "…either pay up or see me in my office after the meetin'." The projectile spittle made it hard sometimes to take him seriously.

"Ten Bucks?" Multiple groans from the peanut Gallery.

This was highway robbery, but it was also the status quo. Bunch of us guys were raised in North Jersey and I know that it is better to *always* run the Pier by Jersey rules. These 'Rules' have been in place long before any of our grandfathers were born. For guys that couldn't come up with ten bucks, they owed Mr. Ryan 30 minutes of free work. A ledger that held the 'balances owed' and the fines paid was kept in public view. The temptation to tamper with the ledger is strong for most. I don't even think about it, being from North Jersey.

Every now and then, an Indian will run off the reservation. Most always, it is someone who thinks we all just showed up here too.

The best part of break time was riding the 'freeloaders' without mercy. Longshoremen have a sense of humor that is uniquely forged from hard labor on the docks.

No ordinary joke will do, it has to cause pain and humiliation. Locker pranks and klutzy equipment set-ups comprised the majority of practical jokes. The craziest thing I've seen in all these years was that short, dark-haired Irishman, Sweeney.

A few months ago, while Mr. Ryan was out for a week, Sweeney thought it would be funny to write fifty bucks onto Tony Pazo's name in the ledger. I know you want to stop here and ask me;

"Is that the former Middleweight contender Tony Pazo?"

Yes, it is.

Tony hadn't been in the ring in ten years but nobody messed with Tony. When his punches started to slow down, his father-in-law set him up here with Priority East Coast. A little while back, Tony and I got into a disagreement about my old route. Mickey told me that the guys upstairs wanted Tony to take over, so I should just let Tony have it. I wouldn't just let him have my route, but I really had no power to stop it.

During the next couple of runs to Baltimore, a few of the customers gave me the stink-eye. I also heard little cracks about how they would miss me, the sarcasm was ample. I did nothing to earn this 'attitude' but there it was. I could smell the noxious burp of the Union from a mile away.

A little while later they just took me off the route,

Mr. Ryan and Mickey took me for beers. They talked to me about how some things could not be helped. The 'Union Rep' that got Tony a job with our firm, also supplied materials to our major shippers. Also, anyone at dock level was a working man and decisions came from 'upstairs'.

I forgot what I was saying about Big Tony, oh yeah; I hated him for a while. That is probably why I didn't say a thing when Sweeney pranked him in the ledger. What made the joke even funnier is that Tony took his work very seriously. Poor guy, he was unaware of the fake debt that he was being ridiculed for. He just never thought to look upon the ledger. By Friday the guys were howling at him. Out of compassion, somebody made sure Tony figured it out and when he did, Sweeney got lit up like the Fourth of July.

In order to keep his job, or his life, Sweeney was made to pay all of Tony's future fines. Consequently, Tony was the fastest driver in the company. No wondering why, there were no financial consequences for earning complaints. Sweeney has paid dearly for this, lesson learned. Sadly, another ten dollar lesson was learned today.

This incident had an effect on anyone who was even thinking about messing with the ledger. There are days when I swear that fuckin' ledger starts to collect dust; nobody touches it except Boss Ryan.

My brother Mickey and I have been working here since our teens, Mickey has done considerably better. I am still on the routes while he is a Freight Boss, his "second" job was Dock Supervisor. There was only room on the books for 5 "Union" positions per pier; every guy on this pier was fighting for one of them.

Because the competition was so fierce, I had to watch Mickey's back quite a bit. By keeping an eye out for Mickey there was a nice trade-off, essentially this meant that I got the primo routes.

A couple of years ago, I was handed the Philly/Baltimore run. I made this route my own. I had developed a numbers game and some small business loans along the route, thanks to Mr. Ryan. I did great for the company and for myself. A report got back to the upstairs people that I started getting an attitude with some of the clients on that route. What a coincidence that it was at the same time they were trying to squeeze Tony into my shoes.

The money is better when you are driving to Baltimore and back twice a week, on top of that, the local runs were static. The same redundant deliveries to the same tired old customers. Some of the clients on these routes were grandfathered in so deep that drivers had to be near-perfect to not earn a complaint. I was grandfathered in too, so they know better than to try that shit with me. I had collections to make in Philly next week, part of it was for Mr. Ryan and another piece was for Mickey. Normally I don't even have to ask for the route, but lately they had Tony P. doing the run.

I took the initiative to spy the bill of lading for Baltimore for Monday and it was huge. There would be an extra truck going and I was so sure about getting it that I didn't even mention it until Monday morning. I really needed to not be on the dock that week, but I knew Mickey would punch my ticket so I wasn't even worried. Another upside to being in a truck, a day of not boring myself to death on the Pier.

No chance for bonuses on the docks, the whole week you were just stuck there until your team started driving again the following Monday. With my luck lately Baltimore would come up again and I would be stuck on the docks. Teams alternate to stay up to date on procedures and mostly so nobody gets burned out. Nothing is longer than a week of loading for the drivers from Team 2.

"Pazo…load number Ten and get down to Baltimore before Five O' Clock." My brother stood at his podium handing out route assignments. Big Tony to Baltimore again, third week in a row. Baltimore was tricky, because the distance by land is substantially less than by sea. This usually allowed for one driver to spend a whole day making one delivery. I think we can all agree that this was a 'primo' assignment.

"Hey Mickey, what gives?" I asked him rather bluntly.

"Ricky, you can't take this one, okay?" I hated when he called me Ricky. That name was cool when I was 13, but I am trying to be Rick now. Even Rich would be okay, not looking to be a "Richard" because, hey, there's no one from North Jersey named Richard. No way.

"Tony, look alive kid…." Mickey was talking past me, I hated that.

I was going have to take this up with him later.

My morning was eventful enough, even though I was stuck at the pier. A load of copper spools arrived; I ran the crane for the duration of the load. Two solid hours not throwing crates. The crane was the best job on the dock, except for Mickey's.

Only four guys were certified for Industrial Lifts, so I got put into the regular rotation. You could smoke and eat sandwiches in the control box, which was air conditioned. It wasn't as nice as a drive to Baltimore, but it did pass the time nicely.

When the whistle for first break went off, I got in step with Mickey; I got in his ear good, too.

"Mickey, I gotta know why I ain't drivin' south right now." I was hot.

He walked with me until we made it around the corner, then he pinned me against the wall.

"You think you're smarter than me kid?" He was hot, too. "Don't you forget kid, I was the first one to kick your ass, and I will be the last one too."

"Mickey, you are passin' me over, I'm your blood!" My rage was welling up; I felt tears arrive at the back of my eyeballs.

"Believe me Rick, I am doing you a big favor, let it go!" One of the rare occasions that I got to be Rick. I could take on Mickey, but the rest of the guys around the dock would come and fight for Mickey so it wasn't worth it.

"Okay, but that won't do it, you gotta tell me why." I could not relent, I was so curious at this point that I considered leaving "sick" and driving down there. How absurd it would be, following behind Tony to see for myself; this great mystery in Baltimore.

"All's I can say is that if I gave you that route, Ryan would have my ass." Mickey meant it too. His voice now had that glint of having been stepped on. Mickey had more to lose than I did, I gave it up.

"Enough said, but I don't like it. You wouldn't either Mick!"

Defeated, I went back to the Pier where I decided to throw up in front of Mr. Ryan. I learned how to throw up on cue back in my 'college years', sometimes it came in handy. He had a serious aversion to vomit, this made for an easy half-day off when well executed.

I had trouble getting my pinky deep enough back into my tonsils. Once the middle finger made it past the molars, I was home free.

With precision timing, as Mr. Ryan carried his bag of corned beef and potato chips I lurched over and let go into the water. Peppers and Eggs, dramatic and colorful.

I carefully placed the angle of the action right in Ryan's view.

"Lomax!" I did it, he was furious.

"Lomax, get off my pier right now!" I wasn't moving fast enough, Mr. Ryan called some help over. Big Pete Morgenstern and Mickey came over to help me away from the docks.

"Sorry Mr. Ryan, I been keepin' it in all morning…." I turned to Mickey and Pete; "Sorry guys, it just came over me…..did I get any on Ryan?" I asked apologetically.

"Yeah, you got close enough." Mickey was even convinced, amazing. Setting his board down, he asked if I was okay and then sent me home for the day. "Take it easy Ricky…you gotta be in tomorrow for the Paper shipment."

"I know. I will be here even if I'm still throwing up." I knew I wouldn't be throwing up.

I grabbed my stuff and walked laboriously to my car, I made sure to move slow and look green all the way out.

Once I cleared the entrance to the Pier, I didn't even turn back towards home. I headed straight for 195 so I could beat Tony down to Baltimore.

The good and bad thing about the Priority ECI trucks was that there was a governor on every engine. This meant that the fastest they could move was at about 67 miles per hour. Tony got a 2 hour start on me so I would have to be moving at 80 to 85 m.p.h. the whole way to even get close. Another factor I had forgotten until now- there was an inspection station just across the bridge into Delaware on Highway 40. Depending on how long the lines were, this would give me almost an hour back. I could make this.

As the miles disappeared under the wheels of my decrepit Pontiac Grand Am, I kept a keen eye out for Tony. If he sees me I will be dead. After getting onto 295 and heading south, I made it to the Delaware border inside of 2 hours. I hadn't seen the Priority ECI truck yet. It was only about another two hours to Baltimore, I would certainly see Tony before that. I had to stop for some food and I had to pee real bad, I stopped in White Marsh. While I was eating and getting back onto the Highway, I saw Tony drive by. This was perfect timing. I could easily stay back behind him, and drive I-95 all the way in.

Once we got near the Baltimore Pier, I got a

little braver. He was now two cars ahead of me. I decided that this was a foolish and paranoid decision I had ever made, coming down here.

I came this far so I knew I was crazy. When Tony got into the city, he made a strange move. He just sat there.

I was officially confused now.

I must have watched that truck for an hour before a Cadillac pulled up behind Tony's truck. A couple of really fat guys, maybe identical twins, climbed up into the truck. Once they were in they sat another forty minutes.

They started driving again and I am sure they spotted me following, I didn't care anymore. As I paced behind them down an access road, the passenger door opened and Tony fell out on to the street while truck was moving at a good clip.

"What da fuck?" I must have repeated this four or five times. The sense of sickness that filled my stomach was palpable. I stayed behind them but I was dizzy from the thought of Tony getting steamrolled by traffic right about now.

Could be me getting the pancake treatment next.

The truck made its way to a warehouse just north of the Glen Burnie Airport. No surprise there, maybe it was air freight?

I had a decision to make; I could call the cops and have these guys busted for dumping Tony out of a truck. I could also try and find out what the hell is going on, which could get risky. I have always pretended to a toughness, really I am just as scared as the rest. Today I would quit pretending and live up to my own reputation, the one I had invented for myself watching all those cop shows growing up.

I walked up to the warehouse office and asked if I could use the rest room. I was still wearing my Priority ECI shirt.

"Public bathrooms are down by the Customs office, around the corner and down two floors." The pudgy senile guard announced.

"Thank you!" I replied. With that, I moved into a good vantage point for observing the truck as it came in.

I walked along the railing and waited at the end of the landing where no one could see me. I saw the door slide open to the freight yard, Tony's truck turned in a long circle before stopping in front of Door #7.

I hopped the railing and ran free to the corner of the yard.

"Ricky…dammit, what the hell am I doing?" The mantra of self-doubt had started.

"Ricky, Ricky, dammit again, Watch your step Ricky." My silent mind was now talking to itself. I was calling myself Ricky! I knew how childish this was, even on a subconscious level.

I could now see as the doors came up, the truck was backing in. The two fat guys got out and went to open the back of the cargo hold.

Now there were two other people in blue jumpsuits working up on the dock. All four of them talked casually as the door started coming down slowly. The men turned and started to walk back out of the doors, as the doors were about halfway down, all four of them were clear of the entrance.

I was now determined to get into that warehouse.

I ducked down and hid for several minutes I couldn't watch to see if everyone had walked out of there. While I was down, I must have been spotted.

When I finally stood up to get a good look, one of the fat guys was right behind me. He had a gun pointed squarely at my neck. I noticed him yet, I remained calm like I had expected to see him there.

"I thought I told you Priority guys to stay the hell out of our warehouse!" He was a spitter too, "Fuckin' Tony didn't know any better, now he knows!" Fat guy one was boasting about hurting, probably killing one of the guys on my dock.

He and the other Fat twin were livid. "You guys aren't supposed to know where these trucks end up; you know what we have to do now?" I suddenly felt a chill, the Reaper was sitting with me and I knew it. "Every time you peep, you get shot, when you get shot, you fuckin' die, friend.

"I know"

As resignation melted my physical plant, I was not really scared anymore like I thought I would be. I was almost relieved that I didn't have to show up for Paper Day tomorrow. Now I know why Mickey said mom and dad didn't want their sons having to work around these bad elements. These tough guys, who have shown me in ten seconds exactly how tough I wasn't. I thought of all the rough scrapes I'd been in and gotten out of through my supposed grit and toughness. In all those memories, all those visions, I never felt a sense of certain finality such as this. Anyone hard enough to push Tony Pazo out of a moving truck in broad daylight surely wasn't worried about the likes of me. As tough as I had been up until now, that wouldn't matter. In a time not long from now, I would begin decomposing. In a situation like this, even boot leather would wither and fade in cowardice.

Once this calm swept over me, the men developed confusion as to which Pier I was from. "You should have never worn that uniform; it signed your death warrant buddy." He was laughing as the sentence trailed off. The others enjoyed a chuckle before I glimpsed a black baton coming at my side at the speed of light.

The second fat guy folded me in half with a shot to the ribs. The pain was tremendous; it hurt so bad that I knew a few of them had to be broken immediately. It felt like was already dying.

"Tell Mickey I just had to know why I couldn't make this run today…I didn't know what was going on here….I still don't."

"Nice story princess" The first fat guy picked up a knife, "You'll be telling it to the bottom feeders."

I was getting scared again. I wasn't afraid to die, but that was before I considered the pain leading up to it.

"You have one chance to get out of here, friend" Which fat guy was talking didn't matter at this point. Some stupid fat guy had my attention, fully.

"Please, I will do anything to get home today…." I was desperate, it definitely sounded like it.

"Start running, towards the South docks." The voice paused for a puff of his cigar, "We won't start shooting until you reach the wall."

He spat a chunk of the butt out and exhaled hastily. "You know what happened to Tony, so we will be aiming for your ass the whole way."

Another blurry voice chimed in, "Wouldn't be right to let you live after killing Tony, he was our friend."

"Don't you ever even think about this place again, got it?"

"Got it." I swear that I was about to start pissing my pants. Fat guy one called out, "Mickey's a friend too, we know who the fuck you are, and the Union rules on this mean we have to give you a chance to either run or defend yourself."

"Deal." I took whatever chance I could to get out, even if it was a slim one.

"You won't survive the climb over the wall, but if by some fucking reason you do…."He was gasping over the cigar for the words, "….you better be smart enough not to talk- Tony talked. Nuff said my friend?" He was talking like a monster and he really emphasized the word "Friend". I nodded to reassure that I heard and understood.

"Once you reach the wall, we get to unload on you, climb that wall as fast as you can…now, GO!"

It took me a hundred years to start running, time seemed to stand still.

I ran at about a ¾ speed and sped up to hit the wall as high as I could, I barely had a hand over the top when the first bullet hit the steel coating on the concrete wall. I would have to jump in the water to get out of here.

There was no hesitation on my part, as I made it over the top and pushed off. I couldn't say how far down it was exactly, it was at least 30 feet down to the surface of the water.

I balled up in order to make it into the bay without hitting the curb.

Once I was in the water, I felt a bullet burning in the flesh of my butt. The water definitely cooled things down but I knew it would be bad. I dragged myself out of the water about half a mile up the shore. I limped in a cowardly stumble towards my car and got in.

I never felt so secure in my life as I did the moment I sat down in that car and locked the doors. I could barely even sit in the seat; my backside was burning and bruised to an extreme.

I had a hard time making it to the Urgent Care. I drove for 3 hours straight, all the way back to Newark before getting my butt looked at. The X-rays of my ribs were negative, nothing broken.

So here I was. I had to make it in to work for the worst day of the week.

My ass hurt, my pretty little face was marked up good, and my ribs felt like someone had scattered embers around inside there. I wasn't happy or comfortable, but I was alive.

How was I going to explain these injuries to Mickey and Mr. Ryan when I was supposedly sick at home all day? Maybe I will keep the souvenir from Baltimore to myself and just say I was in a wreck "on the way home".

It's sort of true.

THE EXODUS OF MARGARET

Our friend Sheila had stopped by to announce the birth of her niece. This was the fourth day she had come by with news of the appalling labor that her young sister Margie had endured. Calmly she went to the liquor cabinet. She drew a glass of Bourbon, after a pause she voraciously took it down. She sighed in a fashion that caused relief to settle upon the entire household.

Her family had grown up with ours, she thought of us as a second family. My father married their oldest boy Mitch to Gladys Barnes down at the Holy Acres. We knew her niece was in poor health, she wanted to make clear the dire situation. For the baby, prognosis was three to seven days, and Margie was wrought with grief at the prospect of watching baby Jessica fade away with every second. Sheila always had a yearning towards the dark mysteries of death.

The Stewart sisters were the first to play 'Witches' which is the equivalent to the male child's 'Army' or 'War'. They formed a coven, for a month or two they had my baby sister Brenda convinced that a spell had turned her blood blue. They showed her the veins in her own wrist while chanting some comically simple Pig Latin. When Brenda saw that her veins were blue, she ran home crying to Mom.

The Stewarts were a tightly wound bunch, the men were permanently dour. The sisters made them all seem a little more human. We all knew the bad luck they had endured and there was a dangerous tension in the air. Today in our parlor, Sheila's face bore a stoic presence that I could almost smell. The fragrance was metallic in nature. My brother Carl, who always liked Sheila, walked over and bowed his head in front of her, trying to inspire a smile.

She did not blink.

He then reached out to comfort her with a friendly embrace, welcoming her to release the emotion that would surely come bursting out. In contrast to his expectations, she receded and shook him off.

Holding back tears, she thanked him. Sheila stepped away toward the door, she stopped and thanked us all again for the spot of drink. My mother walked with Sheila back to the old Stewart house.

That night Sheila went into the barn. She never came out alive.

The Magistrate surmised that she must have

stripped naked, doused herself in gasoline and built a pile of hay under the loft. The bottom floor was erupting in flames as she stepped off the edge of the loft. She fell into a void that helped a noose tighten quickly enough to snap her neck. There she burned toes nine feet off the ground. She perched just high enough that she could not be cut down. So much hay surrounded her that I would have to imagine that she literally sizzled and popped before curling into a black remnant of her female shape. It must have been sight, Sheila burning and all around her the flames gathering strength. She hung there lifeless; neck askew from the spinal alignment, her eyes looking up numbly. She never felt one flame lick against her skin. In some ways, it was the only good luck a Stewart ever enjoyed. Fortune paid off all bad karma with her dying so easily.

When the first firefighters had arrived, she was still hanging. Smoke was slowly emerging from her bones and whatever was left of her charred flesh. The rope held up against the rage of flames in the upper level of her family's barn. Among the many preparations she had made, the most telling of her final acts was to lay a wedding dress on her bed inside the house, its arms folded in a hug. In her tedious and boring life, she had known little of joy. She had never even been laid. At 23, she had returned to the dust, all her bad luck was used up.

She was engaged to Beau Foster since she was 15. They weren't married yet because she was so young. He was drafted into the service when Pearl Harbor was attacked. He wanted to fight and the Navy put him to work rolling chain. Every minute he thought of his girl back home. It was too much for Beau, they had even been waiting until they were married to do the deed. At the start of a war, the end seems a lifetime away. He had been away for four months and already he was homesick with no chance of getting home for a very long time. The ship he was on had just crossed between Australia and the Indian Ocean, he was half a world away. At night, he dreamed that if he could jump high enough, the world would turn underneath and he could land right where she was. Sickening desire took hold, his heart raced at her absence. This despair caused a flurry of demerit notices; Ensign Foster had lost all focus. One night, just before a disciplinary council was to be convened against him, Beau walked off the deck of the ship. He was retrieved by divers and sent home in a box. The War Department delivered his personal effects and dog tags to Sheila at her home. Beau Foster's parents did not want them, or any other reminders of the river of misfortune they were anchored in.

They knew how much Beau loved little Sheila, she was sweet on him too. This hope that was snatched away and given to darkness gave substance to the theory that her 'barn accident' was certainly suicide.

The police had wrapped up the investigation and determined the 'accident' to be a suicide by hanging. The arson was an aggravating factor, not the primary cause of death. No smoke was in her lungs, which meant she did not feel the burning.

This report was met in my household with a sense of disbelief. Sheila was dead, never coming back.

She was unable to redeem the long overdue good luck that was going to come any day now.

Four days later, she was joined by little Jessica.

Margaret Elaine was now the last of the Stewarts, she decided in this moment that she would forever be the last of them.

Margie came to realize the lonely prospect of living on her family land without Sheila. Little Jessica's father was long gone, a million miles away and still running. Some heard that he took work in Alaska to get away from the Stewart curse. The curse seemed ever more daunting with the loss of Jessica. After about ten days, she was tired of being a Stewart. She could not carry on here any longer.

Margie gathered up all the money and valuables hidden around the property, she did not even blink as she drove away from the hill country house. The flames that would engulf the property were still contained in the basement. The firewood pile under the stairs would take care of the rest. With the barn already gone and the house burning down, only an outhouse remained.

Oak Hill was darkened by noticeable degrees in those first weeks following the burning down of the Stewart house. Eventually the old bark peeled off, new growth had begun and the stale history of this filthy burg would resume its glacial pace towards contented simplicity.

The charred pile of boards that memorialized of the Stewart house sang out its smoky aroma for a good distance. The morning winds carried it a quarter mile away over to our house. Three of us wandered over to see if anything was salvageable. There was nothing.

Margie had ensured that nothing would be left behind to mark the fact that her family had lived on that land. After eighty-five years of Stewarts in Oak Hill, nothing remained even so much as a set of initials in a tree. Just the headstones in the local cemetery that seemed like a scoreboard, it showed the utter defeat of the Stewart DNA in this county.

In a few short weeks after the fires, my childhood managed to pack its bags and clear the premises. I planned an exodus of my own, one that included attending classes at Mississippi State. I wasn't going to burn anything down except my past; that had to be done away with. This period proved to be the gauntlet that, once endured, forged my integrity and will to succeed.

I had not seen Margie in the fifteen-plus years since she left Oak Hill.

On a busy November day as I was walking around the campus at State U, I saw her sitting on a blanket with a professor. She remembered me and yelled out.

"Your blood is blue little Brenda!" She got up and hurried to give me an ebullient hug. She introduced me to her husband, Professor Sykes.

"That scared my sister for years Margie!"

Margie went looking for a camera in one of her bags. "Tom Denton, this is Julian Sykes."

Professor Sykes held out his dove-skin hand and limply squeezed an acknowledgement of my grip. "Pleased to meet you Tom, you are the first person she has ever introduced me to."

"Where did you go after the Hill?" I had waited for the answer to this question for years.

"First I went to California and got high for ten years, then I got a job here on campus and that's where I met Julian." She was so positive and happy that I barely recognized her. The time she spent in California must have redressed all her grievances against Karma; she was simply transformed. I think she must have found a butterfly's strength in breaking through the chrysalis to become a whole person. This could have never developed in Oak Hill.

"The Stewart curse has been broken I see!" I gave a punch line of my own, she laughed. I chided her a bit more about the coven,

"You know my blood is still red, some of that witchcraft should have changed your luck."

I was so happy to be talking to her now. I had assumed it would be a painfully depressing meeting if I ever saw her again. This was just the opposite.

She confessed, "Once I took my ass out of Oak Hill I felt like I weighed as much as a feather." Clarity was evident in every word; she spoke so confidently with an innocent joy.

I replied relenting, "My family is still back there, except Brenda, she's in Birmingham with PETA. Go figure"

Margie nodded and said, "Animals would be perfect for her, her blood being blue and all…"

We laughed hard and I took down her number so I could keep in touch. We had dinner and drinks one more time before I was due to leave. When the semester ended, I left State U and moved to

Birmingham to help my sister start an Animal Shelter. We would call Margie occasionally and meet her in Mobile when she could drive out. The joy she caught up with was borne out of every death, every stroke of bad luck and burned down edifice in her history. She never had kids again, she knew the pain of their gain and loss already and that knowledge was murky with despair. I never did go back to Oak Hill, Mississippi. The bad luck was waiting there for me and I didn't want it. I think back to that day Sheila came by to give us the last bad news we would ever hear about the Stewarts. The funny thing about Karma is; it warns like the ultimate harbinger and our lives unwind from its silly knots but no matter how hard you try, luck will find you or leave you on its own schedule, in its own time. When the curse of the Stewarts had been deposed, somewhere in the universe there was another family, taking all the right-hooks from fate. Being counted to eight and standing again, only to repeat in perpetuity.

Thank God, I'm a Denton.

L'élégance de L'ennui

Warm fragrances of yeast and fresh milled wheat wafted out of the open louvers in front of *Les Frais*. The breakfast crowd sipped their coffees and juices without haste as cars motored past this envelope of peace. Far from central Paris, the small café was known for its pastries and baguettes. While the breeze carried an irritatingly harsh level of pollen, rose dust and the sweet smell of lavender from the verdant summer gardens nearby, Nara Davies plopped another cube of sugar into her coffee. Her appointment was for ten minutes ago, she was used to it. The arrhythmic jingle of the tiny bells tied to the door of Les Frais kept her rapt in a comfortable bliss. After half a cup, this was the best coffee she has ever sipped.

A waiter leaned in and set down her petite pastry and fruit tray, leaving a ramekin of whipped butter and cream cheese. Maurice arrived as if he were entering his own lifetime achievement awards ceremony, his attitude and body language held no remorse for his tardiness. Tardiness, she had decided, was a purely American invention. In his mind, Maurice arrived perfectly on time for the appointment. Nara did not feel the strength to bicker over time, or the value of her time with someone so carefree. She wasn't a rude person, but if they were in Chicago there would be some cussing and perhaps an aspersion, or two, cast upon him in regards to his intelligence. She was slowly learning to forget the whole pissing and moaning routine she got by with back home.

Miss Davies gave a good opening salvo when she spoke up about the impractical conditions Maurice had placed on their business arrangement.

"You can't feed the birds with just a bird-feeder; you will need some seed to fill it up Maurice."

Her tone elicited a cold squint from Maurice who began his response by sipping at a very strong black cup of coffee while smoking what must have been the world's last cigarette. He caressed his lungs with its tangy smoke and by doing so; he imposed his own pace on the conversation.

"We need to re-negotiate." His confidence was typical of all Parisians, of which Nara was growing tired. While he spoke onward, she took a moment and imagined an archetypical Frenchman. She wondered if he would argue over his own execution, demanding that the blade is not yet sharp enough for the quality of death he requires. She was starting to believe that the Executioner could never be of French origin; a Frenchman would understand this dishonorable condition of the blade and release the condemned man to his home and comforts until the blade was brought into a proper sharpness and polish. Somehow, she likewise knew that the condemned man would gladly walk right back up there have his head lopped off, just to not lose face. Well, there is joke in there somewhere about keeping face while you are losing your head. Yes, Nara decided that this was a perfect description of Maurice and his fellow countrymen. This opinion by the way; was coming from the most irascible social activist to graduate Fremont College- of all time. Ten years ago she would never have generalized an entire nation like she was doing right now. To say she was becoming world weary might be accurate, but in her heart of hearts that would not stop her from solving the murder of Patr Hoergen.

Three months have passed since Hoergen was found strung up emblazoned upon the television screens of international news services everywhere. Hoergen had been catapulted to a posthumous *celebrite'* due to his very dramatic physical demise. Deaths of such a gruesome nature were not really the kind of cases that local police even wanted to handle. It was the practice of most European capitals to keep denial in play when it comes to wading through the morass of human moral deficiency. Christ, in London you can't even have a gun because the cops ordinarily won't have guns either, talk about denial. Justice at the end of a billy-club was hardly an advance for civilization. The fashion of the Paris police was to obstruct outsiders; this wasn't a new or unique ideal. Oddly, the worst opposition she'd ever faced by local law enforcement was in Muncie, Indiana. Muncie was less than two hundred miles from her childhood home. The irony was appalling at times, she could travel half way around the globe and be received better than in a sleepy backwoods burg the next state over. The two nights she spent in the Muncie City jail taught her a valuable lesson. Do not flirt for clues, ever. Nara was lucky to have survived that lesson but, her desire to solve cases drew her dangerously close to repeating that mistake more than once.

Here she was talking to a witness that could help her finish this stupid murder case and go home, and he wanted to pause for the perfect cigarette.

She waited until he was done before launching into any matter of substance.

The taxi and bicycle traffic was saturating quickly while Maurice put out the first of what would be a half dozen breakfast cigarettes.

"What's to negotiate? Is there something new that I need to know? Don't play me the 'drips and drabs' routine Maurice; spit it out." The rudeness of foreigners was a violation of the quiet conspiracy that pervaded the behaviors of even the very youngest Parisian. Visitors must tolerate the rude impositions, but to protest in even the slightest way was not looked upon gladly. You simply will not get your way in this town. What drew sympathy out of Nara's psyche was, she could see that they do this even to themselves. There's no escaping the elegant boredom of Café Les Frais and the entire city surrounding it.

The discussion would end up going nowhere. Maurice was tight lipped about whatever grand revelation he'd just had. He was an opportunist, Nara knew this.

He obviously has all the information she might need to end this job, naturally he will try to extract every penny for each piece of it.

This was another moment of daydream for her, she pictured back to 5th grade when they went all the way to Chicago to see the Museum. There was a photo-journalism exhibit and the focus of the work was "European Casual".

She thought Paris must be heaven back then. It was so beautiful in pictures; it really was idyllic to most children who would see such exhibits. Those children never smelled Paris, nor had they ever experienced some of the random body odor that can ruin even the shortest of bus rides. Certainly there was enough glamour left in the more ultra-urban pockets, but Paris proper was a pungent collection of raw humanity that went unchecked for over a thousand years. It will continue on that way despite the world's acceptance of deodorant technology. Even Russia has embraced personal hygiene, that shocked Nara above all else. Russians want to please you then they move in for the kill. Nara respected the Moscow code, sure, you could have to kill somebody but that doesn't preclude civility. You could after all, kill somebody just as well after a shot of Vodka as you could before. It was very similar to the guillotine etiquette she had imagined for the imaginary French fellow, flavored with a Russian twist of cruelty. They wanted you to know who was coming to kill you; that was part of the killing process in Moscow.

Hoergen chose to be oblivious to the dangers of being too American. He had been raised in the Belgian consulates abroad, mostly in Washington D.C. and the Philippines. Despite his mother's cautionary tales, he developed that arrogance of selfish claim that can only ascribe to the American culture.

Here she was in that very morass that Paris Metro could not be a part of.

Nara pulled out a slip of paper and wrote down some information for Maurice.

"Maurice, I want you to do this for me and after the investment I have already made, this one is on you." Maurice shrunk immediately, knowing that the fish was about to drop his hook.

"Madame Davies, forgive my stubborn ways...of course I will do this. But! When I do complete this final task, you will pay me the price I asked at the beginning of our arrangement."

"If you could do the job I paid you for already, we wouldn't be here now. I wouldn't be burning fourteen hundred dollars a week staying here, so please, Maurice, stop talking about money. You've been paid already and your results are questionable, in fact, I deserve a rebate on un-delivered services."

Maurice stared her down. How dare she insult him in a public place. Who was she to judge the value of his work?

"Maurice, do it or don't do it, but just stop asking for more money."

"Okay! Enough! I will finish the assignment;

don't expect to ever come to Paris again." With that, the relationship was irretrievably torn. Nara now depended on no one. Hard to see at the moment, that was the liberation she needed.

When she finished walking the six breezy blocks back to the hotel, the urge to take a hot bath swept down her body like goose-bumps.

Her room had been ransacked and all of her research had been either burned or removed. When she pushed the door open, she did not even need to enter the room. She looked at the destruction momentarily and she shrank into a ball on the floor and got very angry. Frustration had been a part of her diet since coming to Paris.

The idyllic playground of her fantasies was in truth, a hell on Earth. This was the end of the case; she was out of resources and out of time on her work visa. It was time to call Mr. Devereaux.

As the night wore on, Nara walked along the wet cobblestones thinking of the next move. If there was ever gonna be a miracle in her life, she needed it now.

She had left a message with Lionel Devereaux, which meant that sometime in the next three days she might hear back. She had no place to stay until the call came from Devereaux.

Maurice went to work finding Nara's next lead, a Swiss grocer who worked near the scene of Patr's slaughter. It was said by other witnesses, that this grocer gave an account of two vehicles pulling up next to Hoergen just before the chainsaws were fired up. The panel vans obscured any view of what actually happened, the coroner surmised that after being opened like a window, his torso released its contents and the whole bloody mess was tied to a cable and dangled from the overpass near Seville De Charvet.

Maurice could not find the man, but he did get an address and a name for the subject. Nara received the information on her laptop while loitering in the B10 rail station. She sent a note of thanks in reply and gathered up her mess. When she made her way to the block of houses where the elusive grocer lived, there were a number of ambulances and police cars outside. She suddenly realized that every lead Maurice came up with, either died or was in jail. She supposed that Henri Poulet had been dead since soon after her message from Maurice.

Stop using Maurice, the voice in her head was repeating it over and over.

No. Maurice was the killer. Nara realized this in the moment that the memory of their last three transactions came back.

Suddenly very afraid, she looked around to see if Maurice was there, somewhere maybe hiding to see her reaction. She continued down back to the rail station she was using during the day for a shelter. She checked behind her several times, she knew for sure that she was being watched.

Maurice was following her with the help a camera mounted on the rooftop of the book store across the street from her former hotel, one block from the B10 station.

He was aware of her movements just as he had been since she got off the plane at DeGaulle. His interference worked so well that he was sad to have to kill Nara. He had enjoyed playing with her mind, sending her after one red herring after another. He was astonished at how long this young, pretty American girl took to find him out.

Nara was putting it together now. As the leads were given out, the subject had already been disposed of. Every one of them was a distraction from the real culprit: Maurice. She knew she was being watched. Instead of trying to lose Maurice, she would lure him close in a public place and use her last line of defense.

The sun was going down now; it had been a long difficult day. Nara had walked about 11 miles today altogether; her feet were swelling up good. Maurice held back as far as it was reasonable to do so, still keeping sight of Nara. He followed all the way to the front of Les Frais, she was sitting down enjoying a butter and brie baguette. While her eyes were intently watching the coffee as it was being raised for a sip, Maurice appeared and sat across from her.

"The game is up Maurice, you're done in." Nara bluffed with confidence.

"I would like to see how this is possible. You are the one who will not be walking away from this table." Maurice spoke with a warmth that opposed his masochistic demeanor, proving to Nara the depth to which he was a pure Psychopathic murder.

"I just want to know, why did you dispatch Hoergen with such malice? He did not deserve that." Nara defended her former associate.

"That wasn't for him, it was for you, so you

would see in advance the very way that I will be killing you tonight, in fact, right now.." He had removed a pistol from his pocket under the small café table.

It was pointed at Nara for sure. She didn't blink, hair on her neck was at 3o,ooo feet and climbing. Her heartbeat sounded as if it were being transmitted through earbuds.

"That may be what you assume is going to happen, you are mistaken." Nara was really bluffing now.

"You stupid Americans don't-"

Maurice was cut off by Nara, "Shut up, Maurice!"

"Maurice, when I lift this cup from the table, an associate of mine will pull the trigger on a high-powered rifle, the only thing I will suffer is your brains on my blouse, not worried about my dry cleaning bill Maurice. Do you hear me?" Nara was almost shouting, the other tables were eavesdropping just enough to sense her anger. They probably assumed this was a couple breaking up in the fashion of most Paris couples, at a Café out near the street.

"I don't believe you..." Maurice didn't bluff as well as Nara, she knew he believed her.

Nara was calmer now, and more intense, "I am going to get up. You are going to hand me your gun and your wallet. When I am gone from here, you won't stand up for at least five minutes, or Paris Metro will be collecting your face off of those louvers, got it?" Maurice blinked and nodded all in one move, he got it.

Nara stood up, collected the gun and wallet and backed away from the table. She waited until she was clear of the rest of the tables and then turned around and walked out of sight. The Metro Police, acting on an anonymous tip from a concerned American tourist, moved in and arrested Maurice for the killing of Patr Hoergen, the Swiss grocer, and two other locals.

Lesson learned, no case is worth four months in Paris.

When she finally made it home to Illinois, she picked up the phone and dialed the Chamber Of Commerce in Muncie, Indiana.

"Hello, Muncie? You ain't got nothin' on Paris, but fuck you anyway…"

Click.

FRIDAY NIGHT

When a story begins, there are supposed to be clues as to where you are standing in the story. It can be a very exhausting exercise, finding those first words. They can be flashed across the first paragraph in a coy fashion. Sometimes the writer wants to be vague, distilling only that spare nugget of information that will leave you where he wants you to be. If I were telling the story of this minute that I find myself in tonight, I would appear to be ignorant of where it is that I am now. I know I was in a box, and that the box was moving. I heard faint sounds, I smelled nothing familiar. I was too bereft of stimuli to realize how long I had been in here. That last thing I can remember is reaching for a light switch inside the bathroom at Shanghai Onion House. I went alone to dinner after work Friday night, I needed a couple drinks before I could go home to the certain perpetual friction of spousal dialogue. I can't honestly say I remember the light coming on or not. I felt no pain, I was not injured in any way but there was the discomfort in my stomach. I was bound up in fashion that kept me from being able to defecate. Unfortunately, I had urinated all over myself and the inside of this stuffed box. A very rough fabric rubbed against my elbows as I squirmed around to the limit of my constriction. I was beginning to think that I was in a railroad car because there was a rhythmic thumping underneath me. I could not be sure because the thumping had turned into a high-pitched hum. The sound was very faint; I must have been insulated quite well in there.

Apparently, I had been sleeping for a while because a large spot of drool had wetted the front of my shirt. I cannot really say I knew anything about what is going on.

Three days ago, I started getting these crazy phone calls from a man saying I had married his wife. He insisted that I married an already betrothed woman. He knew her name, so it seemed strange. I asked my wife is she knew what this was about and she seemed surprised and said "No Idea".

I was in and out of consciousness and feeling faint. This went on for hours as I could not stay awake or swallow anymore. Dehydration was getting severe. In the smallest way, I was able to start moving my knees a little as the ropes have been bouncing with me along these many miles.

The bumps started coming slower until they stopped, and there was a chill coming into the box now. I think the lid was off but I couldn't really tell because my head was tied in a downward pose. As I coughed wildly from the lack of water over the past couple of days, the box was tipped over and I found myself crashing onto the ground beside the truck. Definitely sounded like a forest or a woods of some kind. Secluded.

I couldn't see much because it was dark outside, obviously late in the evening. In addition, whatever light there was around here became too intense for my pupils, as I had been in the dark so long. I still knew nothing of this game.

The man who tipped the box over was now standing over me. He didn't speak; he just looked at me and stood there. After this creepy visual exchange had worn thin, he reached for a long dark object and swung it over my head, which sent blood into my nose and ears. The ringing pain paralyzed me.

I was out for a while again, still groggy.

Now I was in a room and there was a pitcher of water on a table in front of me. I wasn't tied up anymore and I had bandages around my head.

"You wanna die today?" The stranger spoke. I started to breathe a word and he cut me off before the first syllable. "Dying would be good today, yes?"

"I said, do you wanna die today, Mike?" He was clearly emotional at this point, he was shrieking.

"You wanna fucking die… and I am gonna give you what you want!"

The stranger was out of his gourd.

"I am sorry, I don't know your…" I was stopped again.

"You don't need to know my name, my name is Death!" He could not sound more serious.

"Look, can you explain what the hell you're doing to me at least?" I asked knowing there would be more violence. He slapped my head a few times with his hat.

"I told you already what I am gonna do." He was quite excited now; I should not have challenged him.

He brought a cup to me and told me to drink. I was dying to have some of this water. Was it poisoned? Why was he giving me comfort now if he was gonna kill me anyway?

"You are going to stay here until I get back." He demanded; as if I was gonna try to leave. I didn't know where I was, so leaving would be foolish. There are no woods like this around any town in Southern California, I was far from home. Wherever I was, my location had to be separated on all sides by a huge amount of dry desert terrain; there would be no walking out of here.

I heard the faint strains of a radio, somewhere outside the room. Not sure, what song it was but I am sure it was the Eagles playing.

The man left and said nothing of his destination or his return time estimate. I was free except for a shackle around my ankle, and another around my neck, they were both padlocked to a chain that anchored deep into the concrete footer under the floor. I slept again for a while even though I was starving. I was finally able to relieve the build up from not using the toilet by just dropping my pants and letting it go on the floor of this room I was sequestered in. I had little sense of smell left it turns out. I kept a peek out the small plexi-glass window by the door.

A vehicle pulled up outside and I heard my wife's voice, her utter distress was announced and I could tell she'd been drugged. This guy had to carry her in, he stood her against the wall outside the door and removed her handcuffs. She fell into the doorway as he caught her. In a few moments, without provocation she opened her eyes. She stared off blankly and was incoherent. He pushed the door all the way open and she was tossed inside like a bag of trash. The door slammed shut and I heard a bar slide into position on the other side.

Helen was out cold, not responding to my touch. She was still bound for the moment and I had nothing to cut her binds with. It looked as if he'd taped her hands together and just kept rolling the tape around them until it ran out.

"I will make a slave out of you....both of you. And then you will know what it is like!" a voice called out from a speaker in the room.

It was the voice of the stranger.

Several hours must have passed before I heard the door open. The stranger found us huddled together; I had removed the wraps from her hands a little at a time. She was still unconscious. We were dragged outside by a campfire.

"Now the fun begins, are you two lovebirds....READY?" He had the sound of a cuckoo clock all in him.

He took a knife out and shoved it into my lower leg. I screamed out and tried to block the knife from coming down again, it went clean through my forearm. I was sliced pretty good and my hand went numb instantly. I was bleeding out fast; the stranger tied a tourniquet around my upper arm to keep the flow down.

"Why the fuck are you doing this?" I asked, a reasonable question. I thought he was past any real sort of communication so I decided since I was dead already I could goad him up a little.

"That is on a need to know basis, and you don't need to know." He kept the insanity close to him verbally, but physically he ticked like a bomb.

Just then my wife came to. Her vision was not good. She squinted and leered at me, "Michael? What's happening Mike?" She never called me Mike anymore so I sensed her trepidation.

"Sweetie, some guy thinks I married his wife, now I think he's taking out some kind of vendetta against the two of us." I told her what I thought was going on and told her of the box I came here in. She had been rolled up in a carpet and brought here. She didn't know where she was when it happened, probably while sleeping in our old bed.

"You two stop talking, stop talking NOWWW!" He bellowed angrily.

"Dude, who the fuck are you?" I didn't care anymore, my challenge was out there.

I stood up, my pierced calf started dripping down into my socks and I was light-headed. I stared into his face and realized who it was. I hadn't seen Reed Pettit for about 15 years. This was my friend from high school. I knew he wanted to date Helen but they never went out as far as I knew. I deduced that he had obsessed over her. The years probably twisted him into a dangerous frame of regret and paranoia. I wondered inside how many other nameless blameless troubles had brought him to this decision.

What was his desired result? Helen barely could stand me, the love of her life. How was this guy gonna do better?

If he knew how close we were to getting a divorce he might have waited a year or two, but his haste was not to be undone. He meant business. I knew this because he'd been digging a grave just outside the window for a while now. The whole time he was mumbling about how this grave better be deep enough, this grave is for "the dying". Who was cast in that role? Me? Both Helen and myself? Just Helen?

Odd timing. He was engaged in redundancy. Helen and I had signed papers for a separation a week ago. Helen kept the Condo and the Audi. I was living with a friend until a house could be found to move into. Our host must have known at least something about that, if he'd been casing us.

Helen was about to start talking, she explained hoarsely, "Michael, I cheated on you with Reed back in 1997, it doesn't matter much now but I wanted you to know."

"Are you fucking kidding me?" I was flabbergasted. All the gorgeous secretaries I couldn't hire, all the flight attendants invitations that I'd turned down, and for what? Apparently she started our life together as an adulteress. I was sick inside. "We weren't even married a year and you were out screwing the class of 1994?"

This awakening gave me a sickness so intense that I was tasting bile now.

"You couldn't say anything until now?" I asked

"Oh right, like I wanted you to ever find out!" Her anger was displaced, but real. The burns on her wrists were welts now.

I can't believe what I was hearing.

My wife had been shagging this prick behind my back. Who cares when it was, it happened.

I turned on her abruptly. "I hope he kills you first, you dumb bitch."

"Yeah? I hope he does too, then I wouldn't have to smell your rotten breath or hear one more word out of that egotistical mouth!"

Just then, Reed pulled himself out of the hole and went to his truck again. When he came back he was carrying a pistol. He went into a speech that lasted ten minutes or so. "You don't know where you are, you will never make it back to civilization. You two are dead."

He was less emotional now, ten times shakier.

"You two do not have a chance of surviving unless I take you back by vehicle." He was in a position of power, that much was clear.

Three times he cocked and re-cocked the gun. He checked for the round in the chamber, he was breathing hard and covered in sweat. He stood next to the open grave and asked us if we had any last words to say to him.

"This is insane! You're insane! It's been over for

15 years!" Helen yelled. "Is this your plan to win me back? Nice job Romeo." My dumb wife couldn't keep her anger down. I will give her credit, she is a fighter to the last. More than I was saying for myself right now.

"I thought you might say that, let me ask you Helen, WHAT DO YOU THINK OF THIS?"

He put the gun in his mouth and fired. He basically did a bloody Nestea plunge into the hole. In a nanosecond, I felt the calculation of the cold fate he intended for me. His plan was ingenious, now Helen and I were stranded with his corpse. We couldn't leave because the keys were not in the truck. This panic suddenly engulfed me, I kicked as much dirt into the hole as I could with one good leg. Helen just cried with anxiety. She was shaking and sobbing furiously.

I turned around and saw her there. "Well, proud of yourself?" I was upside down with anger. "You've killed us, I hope you're happy"

"Mike, I am so sorry, I am so sorry…" I was about to pass out, she was out of it. What a pair we were. The day turned to night again, I'd found a bottle of water behind the seat of his truck and we drank sparingly.

When the sun came up again we started walking, there were no roads or trails. She wouldn't walk in step with me, but I am glad for that. Considering everything this bitch got me involved in here, I think I would have knocked her clean out.

"You know, I should take you back up there and push you in with that sick dead fuck." I said accusingly

"I wish you would" She was dead in a way already, on the inside.

"This is what you are supposed to get for lying, it just sucks that I have to suffer too." I sounded like a martyr. Well, I was gonna be one.

We walked and walked the whole morning. No more water, no food. I hadn't eaten in a number of days and my pants were not doing very well to stay up.

Scanning in the distance over the rise of a great mound, the Navy boats in the water around Little San Pedro Island shone like a beacon in the water. They were visible at about forty miles. The inner coast was also lightly visible. We were somewhere around Paso Grande, high up in the mountains. It would be another days' walk, I knew I wasn't gonna make it with two stab wounds. After a few miles down the hill, I ran out of juice.

I lay against a tree, where I am now. Helen has gone for help; she is in much better shape than I at this point. I lie against this Douglas fir and hold on for dear life. Will she even come back for me after all this? I hope so, but I surely wouldn't deserve it.

RED CAGE

His arms grew tired holding the torn grocery bag as he stood waiting for the next verbal indication of where to put it down. The smell of the room gathered at the front of his moustache and clung to the nostrils in a brief nostalgia. The kitchen of his childhood came to the front of his memory, almost bringing a smile and then in a second he returned to the attention of Grandma DuBrague and spoke,

"Mrs. D…"

"Yes, Harry?" returning the serve, she seemed anxious to be alone.

"It's Henry, Mrs. D, I have to hurry back to the store, I know we talked about eating lunch together but I see you're not feeling well." Here comes the lob, "Can I help with anything else before I go?"

With that volley began the conversation and obligation that would keep him out of the store for another forty-five minutes. Grandma DuBrague spoke slowly and deliberately even when she knew where her words were going, now she was just stalling to have some company, any company that could help do battle against a long lonely afternoon.

It was not necessarily something Henry minded, but he knew upon returning to the store there would be a look indicating that he had not followed the Boss's instructions.

A few hours earlier, Henry was wrapping fish in the cold room at the store, when Steve told him that he would be on grandmother duty today for the first time.

"Don't initiate conversation or prolong the trip, do what she asks and then get back here, pronto."

"Do you want me to be rude about it?" Henry asked

Steve replied, "Never be rude to my Grandmother, she has the memory of an elephant for rudeness."

"Okay, I will do my best to be quick but courteous." It was clear to Henry that the journey would be most difficult and yet, it was a gem of an opportunity.

The first benefit was time out away from the dusty shelves and floors of DuBrague's - time he would cherish, as he was not much for the repetitive thankless tasks one had to complete in his position. The second part, at least he surmised, was that Steve's grandma was a tender lily pad to a longer, more solid position in DuBrague's management hierarchy.

Of course, she still owned a big enough slice of the company, but her influence did not carry much further than the office door.

Henry was still not clear about what was to be expected by Mrs. Dorothy DuBrague. Common sense kicked in, he'd figured as old and senile as she appeared at times, he could employ an entire "Steve, she's not remembering that right" routine, for whatever complaints that may arise from his short visit in the DuBrague's family home that afternoon.

On his way back to work, Henry passed by the old P.S. #14, he saw the kids playing some hybrid game of basketball and dodge ball. They celebrated this recess with childlike abandon, which inspired young healthy howls to seep through the chain-links.

The playground still had the rusty swings and the bent steel cage that rested on springs next to the merry-go-rounds. The kids all used to use that as a "fort" during games of ditch'em or hide and seek. Sometimes in the summers, we would trick new kids to step in there and lay down, after a few seconds when the heat came up; it would liven up their epidermis to a pink welt.

That cage looked different today, maybe newer than it used to be. He was curious if it had been painted recently but not being of very much concern about it, Henry continued determinedly back to DuBrague's.

Upon reaching the back door of the store, Steve called out, "Is that the boy back from Grandma Duty?"

"Yes Boss!"

Steve again loudly, "… come up front, I have

customers right now."

When Henry got to his side, Steve whispered from the crack of his mouth that it was a job well done. "She likes you Harry, you have such a sweet face…" he imitated her perfectly, the way only a relative could.

"When she gonna start to remember my name?" I joked, because I knew that answer was never.

"She never liked anyone I've sent over there… You? She likes you. Go figure, I can't stand you most days." Steve was being a bit of prick about it but it was, after all, his world.

For Henry to get the idea that he had become any more important after this favor well done, was unlikely. Being a contrarian would only further exacerbate the embodiment of fermenting tension that everyone along Haskell Street knew as 'Stevie Deebs'.

"When these customers die down I want to go take a little break, maybe a power-nap." Steve was sounding a bit worn from the long day at the family shop. Henry was wise enough to see that when Boss asked for a break, one should generally drop whatever-the-fuck it was they were doing and just fill-in for him.

Steve was famous for taking little naps during a day, never more than 30 or 40 minutes. It was a small price to pay to keep the peace, so Henry obliged him easily before waving off the boss.

Henry exhaled and nodded, "I got this."

With that, Deebs slid behind the crude curtain made of old bed sheet and safety pins and let out a groan of relief. Most likely, he was dreaming of horse races while he slept like a corpse on the double-sized cot behind the aquariums.

Henry turned down the radio in the office as the money was counted a second time. He reached for a paper than had been used repeatedly to guard the carbon. Mrs. Deebs needed a copy too, probably to sneeze into because she couldn't read a deposit slip or any other business document. Her eyesight had declined significantly, which is why Steve never let her walk home alone. Some would say she's been a victim of luck, good and bad. She happened to marry the founder of the first deli and drugstore in city. Twenty-five years into a pretty good marriage, on her 44th[rd] birthday, her husband Carl passed away in his sleep. Steve's father, their only son Francis drowned at a cousin's birthday party. He had been drinking like a fish, too bad he was unable to swim like one. The tragic accident happened because the death of his father was too much to take. Frankie went for a cigarette out by the pool alone, a week before Christmas, 1974. The whole family was inside; when Frankie was gone for a while, someone went after him.

There he was in the pool, it was very cold outside and no one could jump in to get him out.

When help finally came, little Steve stood there with the indifferent curiosity of a 3 year-old.

While grieving these events, Steve's mother suffered a complete emotional collapse. At first she went to a hospital, when she could stay there no longer it was recommended she enter a convent. She had been unable to shake the grief to a degree that she was a danger to herself and others. The nunnery proved a soothing balm, though she did not live very long after, she had regained her sanity and was able to contribute in meaningful ways. During the holidays while she was out tending the grounds, she fell ill. A severe pneumonia had accumulated in her body, slowly and over a very long period. The depression and the mental strain of losing her husband was unbearable, not to mention the effect of watching helplessly as he froze to death. Lifeless and staring back from the bottom of a pool, it would be a tight wrench on anyone.

Steve had no family left except his grandma; he had never gone around the rest of the family after the drowning. The rest of the extended relatives viewed Steve as a bad luck omen. It was the very slim margin of gypsy blood showing itself like a breeze hitting a flag.

Steve was 6 years old when he went to work in the store and for ten years, he was Dorothy's only assistant. She taught him well enough to pretend he runs things. If it were not for Sal and I working behind him, the place would be out of business in a week.

"September fourteenth nineteen…" The ink went dry, and then hesitantly resumed its flow, "nineteen ninety-eight, there, deposit is done." Henry spoke to reassure his accounting. It was a subtle technology, talking to himself.

People often caught him in a state of mumbling, it was a defense.

After closing up the rest of the store and finishing the stupid, redundantly un-necessary tasks included in that, Henry set his sights on going home. Last step was walking to the drop box at Firstfield Bank. Walking mindlessly, he could barely remember placing the pregnant bank bag into the slot. He actually turned around to double check. Turning back knowingly, scratching his head and then strolled on a few more blocks towards Barney Parkway and West Plum.

From inside the small studio apartment a muffled beeping sound called out into the worn out wood-paneled hallway.

The message machine was filled to capacity.

Turning the key, he decided to clear the alerts but he wouldn't listen to any messages tonight. His heart and brain were drained already.

If the machine was that full, then that meant there was someone collecting on a long abandoned debt or at best, a friend or family member once again desperate to get a hold of him to borrow something, usually money. Henry could barely get to the end of a newspaper with the evenings getting shorter and shorter, mostly from the ever-expanding process of closing up the store.

Sorting dimes? Yes, sorting dimes. The customer's change needs to be shiny. Rusty dimes go to the bank.

"Another day, another fifty cents." Henry entered his sanctuary with the same basic disgust that all people develop for their shabby routines. A good start was letting out a huge sigh, followed by some moderate cussing and cracking his knuckles. Let us not leave out that a vigorous ruffling of his hair. This procedure seemed to relieve those last nuances of stress. This kinetic poetry made the preparation of a sparse evening meal seem easier to get through. A sort of haiku written in scrambled eggs and Doritos.

The din of a small radio from the bathroom whispered into the dusty space like the voice of anonymous company.

Henry gave a bit of food to his hamster named "Giraffe", and opened the Sports page to read some box scores. No team mattered to him more than any other did, but certain players caught his ire. It was always nice to see that one of them went 0 for 4 and lost the game. Mike Piazza was one of these players and on that night in particular, the hits line read bad news, Piazza - 2-4, HR, 2B, HBP.

The Mets lost. Was this paper from today? This week? Defiantly fighting off a yawn, the intentional beaning of Mike Piazza required a howl.

"YESS!" Henry bellowed.

An upstairs neighbor let out a muffled warning, announcing his need for quiet. Henry hated that guy. More than once, Henry sent a mysterious pizza to his apartment, cash delivery.

Determined to express the end of this current emotion, he brought the intensity down and smiled. "At least that stubble-bearded bastard got beaned." The king of alliteration talking over here.

The night passed in a quick series of news articles that Henry pondered while the Cuban radio station crept along evenly. Soon tired, he reached for a thick red blanket and clapped the lights down. Henry laid there awake for ten minutes and attempted a meditation to organize the next days' errands, chores, and duties.

"How nice it would be to not work…" A bustle of traffic moved light and shadow over the room from the window on Barney. The hill at the bottom of Barney Blvd. sent those headlights all over his walls, even on the third floor.

One of the cars honked. His opponent honked back. With that, Henry could no longer keep his eyelids open and he quickly fell into slumberdom.

Henry's consciousness was a barren field of unmet expectations, disappointed mentors, and dreams not yet exciting enough to pursue.

He slept as the cabs and cars on Barney became a metaphysical conveyor belt. An occasional horn sung out and bounced upward between the buildings until, at a whisper level, it blended into the soft Cuban rhythms with all the ease of a big-toe bunion in a tight loafer.

Henry was dreaming…

A crowd of seagulls gave chase to a strand of salty air that laid out in front, as he walked down the sloping beach towards the lights of some pier that never seemed to get any closer to him. A mime with a bony frame and whiteface was doing his best robot routine on the boardwalk, people were gathered around and having a good time. He lifted a scarf from an unknown pocket in his coat and threw it in the air; it turned into mist and then flames. Nice trick. None of the usual smells accompanied this listless adventure, instead of seaweed and dead fish buried in the sand. As Henry walked, he could detect warm marshmallows and coal burning nearby.

Floating through his dream, Henry walked

along an overcast winter beach. Before too long there was a large warehouse building just a few blocks away from the frontage road. Uninviting to say the least, foreboding even.

Setting down his ripped umbrella on the bench near a bulky fountain that bubbled its frothy report in a low whoosh, he felt a colder chill seeping in. A breeze caught his whiskers and renewed the motivation to keep walking.

He walked further into the Main Street view as a wet crosswalk appeared. There were birds flying amongst the light spray of mist that could instantly break into a downpour. The crisp air hung upon his skin as he paced with confusion.

The signs that usually read 'Walk' and 'Don't Walk' were flashing a message from his subconscious depths. The letters got blurry the more he tried to focus but he could make out-

"Red Cage" The sign resumed its "Walk/ Don't Walk" pattern but the message was clear.

Suddenly the dream gave way to absurdity and there were puffy grey and orange clouds beyond the meager coastal skyline, a tedium of two-story shops and buildings.

As he lay dreaming in this bizarre scenario, a sound began to creep in to his dream from the upper consciousness. A quarter mile from Henry's apartment, the whistle from a factory grimly announced the end of a long-shift as Henry sprung up out of bed. In his nostrils, remained the coal and marshmallows from the lucid dream he was alive inside of just moments ago.

He rose from his rest to seek out something

cold to drink, the foghorn from what sounded like 'The Love Boat' still reverberating through his modest apartment. In the cool of the shadowy pre-dawn hours, a mild chatter from the street below bounced around in his ears. Henry decided to stay up and read the paper again and have a pot of coffee.

The haze from the dream hung on him for most of the morning as he went about the routine that became his life these past 15 years. Wake up around six, feed Giraffe, bathe, run the Bissell over the rugs and then iron a shirt for work.

After fifteen minutes of Channel 6 News, it was time to head to work.

A deliberate plan to walk past the playground formed, along with a trip by the library as soon as he could get free from the store. Today would be a half-day for the simple fact that it was Steve's day to go to the track.

For Steve, half the day would be driving down to Sand Bar Downs and back. Win or lose, Steve always came back happy. Gambling was an elixir that Steve imbibed, a spirit only found in the 85 miles of white stripes that fell into the mouth of his crappy Mustang II.

As Henry had predicted, the morning flew by and there was hardly any business going on so they did not even have to do a deposit. This way Steve got a few extra bucks to go to the track with, off the books.

It was a happy day so far, Henry was going to check out the Cage at #14 and there would be enough time to still drop by the library. Maybe there would be enough time to grab a sandwich from Greco's.

The mystery of the Red Cage was enough during daylight, now he was dreaming about it at night too. The afternoon passed sweetly, time did not drag or fly by. During a visit to the library, Henry was able to find out that the red rusty cage had been a gift from a sister school in France. The steel was forged in Liverpool, the workers traveled here from Paris to assemble it during the school's 20th anniversary, 35 years ago. This rusty idol has sat in the playground for most of Henry's life.

After lawsuits and a perpetual occurrence of pranks, the administrators decided to seal the cage. The Door of the cage was set on hinges and those hinges were welded to the body of the cage. No one had worked open the door in 15 or 20 years; it was sealed by rust and corrosion. Henry wanted to see about cracking that rust apart to open the cage door.

Something from his dream told him to concentrate and figure this out, he was mumbling like a rocket... For some subconscious reason, there was a mandate on getting in that cage. It took almost a week to develop a good plan.

The following Friday, after closing, Henry jumped the outer fence at P.S. #14. He made his way to the playground feeling a little like James Bond. He hid next to the water fountains to see if anyone was around. Taking a small bottle from his coat, he sprayed a mist of calcium-lime remover up and down the doorframe of the cage. The dripping caused a discoloration on the asphalt under the cage. Henry had not planned on multiple trips or cleaning up. This was bad. The door was supposed to just breeze open so then he could climb in. Nothing ever goes right, have you noticed?

This small miscalculation made sure that now he would have to finish this project immediately. He took a chisel and a small 2 lb. sledgehammer and bore into the iron flesh of the door. It took around two dozen blows to free the length of the door from its rusty grips. The door swung open freely.

Henry lifted himself up onto the surface of the grate. Upon standing up inside the cage, the door swung shut behind him.

As a sense of triple déjà vu took hold of him, the yellow Beetle from his dream was driving down the street in front of the school.

In a panic, he tried vigorously to get the door back open. The sharp edges from the rusty door tore into his skin and left cuts deep enough to burn with immediate infection. The Beetle honked again and sped away down toward the next block.

The panic proved too much, he ran himself ragged trying to get out of the confinement. He felt his face getting warm and his sight went purple, then he collapsed onto the grate that was the floor of the cage.

When he came to, there was a security guard standing over him. The Security officer had pulled him out of the cage and the two of them were awaiting paramedics.

Henry did not want to wait for the medics so he asked the guard to please go get him some water.

"I don't think I will be able to stand up without

some water, feeling kinda dizzy…." Henry humbly tried to stand, quickly demonstrating his inability to walk.

When the guard walked off around the corner, Henry stood up bolted from the yard. He ran five blocks without looking back.

Back in the apartment he leaned against the inside of the door and exhaled about five times a second. Leaning over with hands on knees, he sighed with a groan.

The radio was in a state of repeat commercials, no news. The wounds were seeping rust and blood. The news came on and Henry could barely pay attention, he was so gassed. The lead story was being read in a panic, warning residents near the east coast to stay inside and lock their doors. The alert also said that boarding up windows was a good recommendation. "Reports from the Tri-State area indicate sudden heat waves moving through most major towns and cities.

When the wind broke through the windows, Henry jumped behind the kitchen counter. A hot flash shredded the room before the eye could catch up with it. In a minute or so after the flash, a dense fog rolled in. The curiosity was hard to contain but Henry felt that if he didn't get into shelter soon there would be trouble. He opened the fridge and pulled out the racks, food went everywhere. Food is no good to you when you are dead so he climbed in and it was tight but he could use the shelves on the door to pull it closed. His instincts saved him; a second later, the place he had been sitting was crushed by part of the upstairs apartment, which fell into his living room. Once everything had settled, he forced the door open and pulled himself out. He was in the lobby of his building, three floors down. Not thinking too hard about it, he ran to DuBrague's to see what was going on over there. There was Steve, opening up the shutter to get in; he'd been turned back by Highway patrol. They went in and pulled the shutter down.

"I think we've barely made it, some crazy shit's going down out there." Steve panicked right along with him.

"Steve we gotta check on Dorothy…" Henry surprised him by being slightly more thoughtful than, well, her own grandson.

"I don't think phones are working, that shit got melted no doubt about it, what can we do?"

We might have to let that go, if we wanna be sure of making it outta here alive." Steve followed, he was being pragmatic, inhuman but pragmatic.

"I ain't opening that shutter for a week, whatever is alive after will be weaker and more tired than us."

"Right, I agree…" Henry assured him of a solid unconditional loyalty. The boss started to cry a little, "She's probably a goner already…" Henry let him off the hook for being a selfish prick that wouldn't go check on his grandmother during what appeared to be an apocalyptic storm.

"I wonder what the hell is going on out there…" Steve was so nervous that he was saying the same thing repeatedly. "Let's check the radio again."

Henry brought the radio up to the counter; he turned it on and scanned for anything.

"Whatever news we get will be bad news, I just

hope we can make it through the looting." Henry was also a little pragmatic.

That shutter door ain't coming up for King Kong; it is bolted solid in five places. They both knew it.

"Just trust me that we don't want to know what is going on as long as we are safe in here, until better news comes or we run out of food…" Henry finally got on board with Steve and said, "Then it will be the best possible week we can have, I will get out the brisket and peppers, you get us some bread, boss?" Henry liked ordering the boss around.

They sat down and ate more beef brisket sandwiches than was appropriate for an occasion such as this. Any one of these could be their last meal; therefore, they must all be banquets of the highest order.

"The radio came on!" Steve yelled from the front. Henry hurried up there.

"Reports of high radiation and a shockwave from an invisible explosion off the coast of Virginia tonight. Also over ten thousand fatalities across the eastern seaboard." The reporter was still nervous with chatter.

"Officials relate this to a message received by the Pentagon earlier this week, the message which has now been released to the press was this," the reporter's voice went stoically plain and monotone for the reading of the message:

"STAY OUT OF THE CAGE NO ONE MUST ENTER THE CAGE"

Henry suddenly had the pangs of knowledge that it was himself who set this crap in motion. How could he know there were consequences for acting on stupid dreams? Nobody could talk Henry out of the guilt that he was building in his heart. He confessed to Steve what he'd thought was going on. He listened and when Henry was done he just said, "Whatever happens now, don't ever repeat that"

"Even if you find out later that you have nothing to do with this, you must be quiet about that, people will be not so happy with you for causing this." Steve was too pragmatic for Henry's taste.

"No, I am gonna go and find out what is going on, I did this and I want to help any one that I can…" Henry and Steve knew he would be killed quickly outside but Henry didn't care, he was resolved to his guilt. Gypsy guilt sucks. Just living around these people, he picked up enough superstition to recognize a little gypsy in himself.

When the door rolled open, the streets were back to normal, it was as if nothing had happened.

Whhhaaaaaaapp! Henry snapped awake. A newspaper slapped down on the counter where Henry was drooling in a snooze, his head on its side as he snored loud enough to summon Steve, who had been sleeping on the cot in the back and was now standing there.

"Have a nice nap errand boy?" Steve asked

The dream was deeper than Henry had thought, he had only slept for forty minutes but somehow he had experienced a week's worth of time in his dream. This was bizarre, Henry could not see Steve following the ins and outs of the dream, he decided to keep it to himself. The day was just about over so they closed up shop, Henry went home. Funny that in reality there were no messages on his machine.

The machine full of messages, how silly? Alone, that should have been evidence that he had been dreaming.

As he opened the paper, he saw that on the front page of the Sports section there was a huge picture of a ball bouncing off Mike Piazza's arm.